LITTLE MISS WISE'S
Winning Walk

Original concept by Roger Hargreaves
Illustrated and written by Adam Hargreaves

MR. MEN   LITTLE MISS

MR.MEN™ LITTLE MISS™ © THOIP (a SANRIO compal

D1514497

Little Miss Wise's Winning Walk © 2014 THOIP (a Sanrio company)
Printed and published under licence from Price Stern Sloan, Inc., Los Angeles.
First published in France 1998 by Hachette Livre
This edition published in 2015 by Dean, an imprint of Egmont UK Limited,
The Yellow Building, 1 Nicholas Road, London W11 4AN

ISBN 978 0 6035 7197 8
63577/1
Printed in Great Britain

Do you know anyone as wise as Little Miss Wise? I imagine not.

Little Miss Wise is as wise and sensible, or sensible and wise, if you prefer, as anyone I know.

Every morning, Little Miss Wise brushes her teeth being careful to use exactly the right amount of toothpaste.

Not a millimetre too much, not a millimetre too little!

And every morning, Little Miss Wise has a very wise and sensible breakfast in her kitchen.

Do you think that she puts lots of jam on her slice of toast?

Not at all. A small amount of jam is wise and sensible.

And every morning, Little Miss Wise takes a walk. Not too short. Not too long. Not too fast. Not too slow.

She also always goes the same way, so that there is no risk of her getting lost.

And it was while she was on one of these morning walks that she met four of her friends.

"Good morning, Little Miss Wise," said Mr Bump. "Come with us to see Little Miss Star. We're going to have a skateboarding race!"

"A skateboarding race?" exclaimed Little Miss Wise. "Are you sure that is a sport that will suit you, Mr Bump?" she asked wisely. "And as for you, Mr Greedy," she added, "don't you think you might break the skateboard?"

"Well enjoy yourselves," she added. "But I prefer to walk. I find it much less dangerous."

And she continued on her way.

Not long after, the competitors in the race were ready at the starting line. Little Miss Star was just about to start the race when she noticed that someone was missing.

Can you spot who was missing?

Yes, Mr Greedy. But they didn't have time to wait for him.

"On your marks ... get set ... go!" cried Little Miss Star.

Mr Bump's skateboard was off at full speed and its poor owner soon found himself wobbling all over the place. He found it very difficult indeed to stay on his board.

So difficult, in fact, that …

… the skateboard continued the race without its owner!

WHEEEE!

And landed just behind Little Miss Wise as she wisely and sensibly continued with her walk.

The skateboard …

… continued the race with a terrified Little Miss Wise on board!

"Help me!" she cried, as she hurtled down a hill at full speed.

Mr Busy was in the lead and he was already at the slalom.

"Tra la la!" he sang as he weaved between the obstacles with great ease and at great speed. "I'm sure to win!"

WAAAAH!

Little Miss Wise, still perched on the skateboard, was the next to attempt the slalom.

Wisely, she closed her eyes …

… and crossed the finish line with a bump, taking Mr Greedy's finishing flag with her, and …

… landed right in the middle of the end-of-race feast.

Or what was left of it.
Mr Greedy had been there earlier, you see.

"Little Miss Wise has won the skateboarding race!" announced Little Miss Star.

All the friends danced to celebrate Little Miss Wise's victory. Although not everyone. Look carefully. Somebody seems to be missing.

Yes, Little Miss Somersault was not in the mood for celebrating. She was feeling rather cross because normally she won every race.

And since then, do you think Little Miss Wise takes a skateboard with her on her morning walk?

Most certainly not.

But she does wear a helmet and knee pads, just in case!